STABLES

Totally unbalanced and unable to stop herself, Poppy did a complete somersault over Henry's neck in awful slow motion. As the rest of the class broke into giggles, she found herself sitting on the sand with Henry gazing down at her, tickling her cheek with his bristly whiskers.

SUNSHINE
STABLES

COMING SOON:

SOPHIE *and the* SPOOKY PONY

GRACIE *and the* GRUMPY PONY

SUNSHINE
STABLES

POPPY and the
PERFECT PONY

OLIVIA TUFFIN

ILLUSTRATED BY
JO GOODBERRY

nosy
crow

FOR MY BROTHER AND MY SISTERS AND ALL OF THE OTHER NHS HEROES.

First published in the UK in 2021 by Nosy Crow Ltd
The Crow's Nest, 14 Baden Place, Crosby Row
London, SE1 1YW, UK

Nosy Crow and associated logos are trademarks and/or registered
trademarks of Nosy Crow Ltd

978 1 78800 793 1

A CIP catalogue record for this book will be available from the British Library.

Printed and bound in the UK by Clays Ltd, Elcograf S.p.A.

Papers used by Nosy Crow are made from wood grown in
sustainable forests.

1 3 5 7 9 10 8 6 4 2

MIX
Paper from
responsible sources
FSC® C018072

www.nosycrow.com

CHAPTER 1

Poppy smoothed down the soft green tweed of the hacking jacket, admiring her reflection in the dusty tack-shop mirror. She liked the way the tweed complemented her hair and eyes. It was perfect!

"Mum, look at this!" Poppy called. Her mum was studying a list, ticking off the things they needed to get for pony camp. There were still a couple of weeks to go, but Poppy couldn't wait to get everything organised!

"Oh, that's nice." Mandy, the owner of the shop, appeared beside Poppy. Poppy knew Mandy well. She liked to go to the shop each week just to look at all the saddles, the brightly coloured rugs, different sorts of bits ... and to breathe in that special tack-shop smell! Mandy was funny and chatty, and sometimes if the shop was quiet she let Poppy practise putting bridles together and would make her a hot chocolate.

"But that jacket is really for high-level competitions," Mandy continued. "I'm not sure you'll need it at Vale Farm."

"Yes, that's lovely." Poppy's mum joined them and stroked the jacket before picking up the price tag. Poppy saw a frown flit across her mum's face and her stomach dropped. She knew that look. "But I think Mandy's right, it's probably a bit much for pony camp."

Poppy nodded.

"OK," she said in a small voice. She would have to put the jacket on her wish list, something to save up for and wear at her first high-level competition with Silver Shadow!

"Ooh, look what I've found!" Mandy said cheerily, placing a pile of brightly coloured clothes on the counter.

Poppy tried to look enthusiastic as her mum rifled through the garments, a relieved expression on her face, and Poppy noticed the sale stickers. There were garish bright-pink jodhpurs with funny squiggles down the side, and a purple jumper covered in glittery sequinned horseshoes. She was grateful her mum was kitting her out for camp as she knew how expensive riding clothes were, but as her mum held the pink pair of jodhs up against her with an approving nod, she felt her heart sink. She'd hoped for canary-yellow breeches, butter-soft leather boots and tan gloves, just as in her books.

"We'll take these!" Poppy's mum said happily. "Thanks, Mandy."

"Lovely!" said Mandy, ringing the pink jodhs through the till. "They'll be just fine for camp. I know there's always lots of fun and games going on, and the beach ride too. You wouldn't want to be wearing a posh jacket." She looked kindly at Poppy.

Poppy tried to swallow her disappointment, and smiled instead, pushing a few strands of her blonde hair behind her ear.

"They're brilliant. Thank you."

"Do you know Elaine Sanderson who owns Vale Farm?" Poppy's mum asked Mandy.

"Lainey?" Mandy replied. "She was only ever called Elaine when she was eventing. Yes, I do. She's ever so nice! Did you know she jumped round the Badminton three-day event? You're going to have a brilliant time, Poppy – her camps are very popular. It was a great idea of hers, opening up the stables."

Poppy started to feel a little better. She'd been looking forward to camp at the local riding school for months – she couldn't let the wrong jodhpurs spoil it now.

As her mum continued to chat to Mandy, another girl came into the tack shop. She was taller than Poppy, with a swishy ponytail that she flicked over one shoulder. Her mum held a list too. To Poppy's growing dismay, the girl headed straight for the jacket – *her* jacket – and slipped it on over her T-shirt, doing a twirl in front of the mirror.

"Lovely," said her mum. "Pop it in the basket."

As the girl and her mum came near the till, adding in some scarlet hair ribbons and a gorgeous gold tie, Poppy grabbed the bright-pink jodhpurs and threw them into a carrier bag, hoping the girl hadn't noticed. She wasn't quick enough with the purple jumper though. The girl laid the beautiful tweed jacket out on the counter, giving it a little stroke, before picking up the awful jumper between her thumb and forefinger as if she couldn't *bear* to touch it.

"Here," she said, her nose wrinkling, "you forgot this."

"Thanks," Poppy muttered, stuffing the jumper into the now bulging bag. She wanted to say something about how she loved the jacket too, but instead she put her head down and scurried after her mum.

In the car on the way home Poppy pulled her

battered copy of *The Manual of Horsemanship* from her bag, a present from her gran a couple of Christmases ago. Poppy read it every single day and even took it to school so she could study it during break times.

She turned to her favourite page, which showed a girl riding the most beautiful grey pony, so similar to Silver Shadow. The girl was wearing a tweed jacket just like the one in the shop and cream jodhpurs, with a navy riding hat and beautifully polished boots. Not a squiggle or glittery horseshoe in sight. Poppy never imagined pink jodhpurs when she dreamed about her grey pony. When she was riding Silver Shadow, everything had to be *perfect*, just like the girl in the picture.

"You coming to the rec?"

Evie, Poppy's best friend, linked arms with her

as the bell rang on the last day of school. The warmth of the sunshine hit the girls as they bounded down the steps. For Poppy, the summer holidays now stretched ahead full of promise and pony adventures. She couldn't wait!

Poppy shook her head. The recreation ground – where everyone hung around after school – was fun, but there was somewhere she needed to be.

"Another time," she promised her friend.

"Ponies?" Evie grinned and Poppy nodded and gave her a quick hug before she hurried off.

The grey was waiting in his usual spot as Poppy made her way along the now familiar path. He lived in the fields surrounding Vale Farm, which was on the edge of town and where camp would be held.

"Hi, boy!" Putting her bag down, Poppy reached up and stroked the silken strands of Silver Shadow's forelock, smiling as he breathed his lovely warm pony breath on to her cheek.

"Not long until camp!" She leaned on the fence as the grey pony nibbled at her ponytail affectionately. "And I just *know* Lainey's going to pair me up with you! We can canter and jump and we'll be the perfect team. You and me, forever." She planted a kiss on the pony's pink muzzle, his ears flicking back and forth as if he was really listening to her.

Poppy didn't *actually* know what the pony was called, but Silver Shadow suited him perfectly and he came when she called that name. He was the most beautiful grey pony, with a smattering of darker flecks around his velvet nose and big eyes. His coat was almost pure white but Poppy knew that you never called a white pony white. It was always grey.

They had come across each other by chance. Poppy had taken the long way home one sunny evening and – like something out of a dream – there he was, peering over the fence, his ears pricked. It was as if he had been waiting for her. Now she always took that way home. She'd think about him all day at school, doodling pictures of him across her workbook, writing poems about him in her lunch break, planning to ride him for the first time just like the girl in *The Manual of Horsemanship.*

They shared a special bond. Sometimes Poppy stroked him and chatted about her day, and other times she simply curled up on the grass and watched him graze, lazily swishing flies away with his tail. She never gave him treats because Lainey, who was sometimes in the fields, had asked her not to, and Poppy knew from her books that too many treats could cause colic. Her heart thudded a little faster at the thought of Silver Shadow falling ill.

Lainey would often give Poppy a cheerful wave. "Here to see the ponies again?" She'd laugh and Poppy would nod and smile, but there was only one pony she was there to see. Even without knowing his real name, let alone having ridden him, Poppy knew he was the pony for her.

CHAPTER 2

"Are you sure you want to sleep here? You can just come up every morning, if you'd rather?"

It was the first morning of camp and Poppy's mum had just pulled up in the car outside Vale Farm. She leaned across to give Poppy a big hug and Poppy hugged her back, keeping the pony-camp booklet clutched tightly in her hand as she did so. She had studied it from cover to cover, soaking in all the information.

Vale Farm ran week-long riding camps throughout the summer. The camps were called Sunshine Stables and they were so popular that there was a waiting list of girls and boys from town who wanted the chance to ride and care for a pony as if it was their own. There were dressage and jumping lessons and hacking and, the best bit of all, a beach ride! Poppy had often seen groups of ponies and chattering, happy riders heading down to the wide sandy cove. She longed to canter along the beach, darting in and out of the shallow waves. And now, finally, she would, and on her dream pony!

"Definitely," she said, hoping she sounded a little more confident than she felt. She sat back in her seat and looked at the bright cover of the booklet. A girl, being nuzzled by a beautiful pony, smiled back at her. "I'll be fine." She pointed across the cobbled yard, which was already busy with pony-camp kids and their parents. "I think that barn over there is where we stay."

"Looks a little draughty," said her mum. "I hope you'll be comfortable."

Poppy watched the chickens scratching around under stable doors, and a couple of cats sunning themselves on the mounting block. And then she had to look twice as a sheep pushed open the little gate from one of the paddocks and sauntered across the yard, heading straight for the pile of suitcases and bags! Through the car window, she heard gentle whinnies and the clip-clop of ponies' hooves mingling with the excited chatter of the other children. She didn't care about being comfortable. She'd dreamed about staying at Vale Farm for months and finally she was here!

"I'm sure you'll have a lovely time, but you can always call me if you're feeling homesick," added her mum.

Poppy smiled. "I know. Thanks, Mum."

They only lived down the road but she didn't

want to miss a second of her time with Silver Shadow.

"OK," her mum said. "I'll get you all booked in."

Stepping out of the car before her mum drove off to park, Poppy plucked at the sleeve of her purple horseshoe jumper and looked around. Taking a deep breath, she took a few steps towards a friendly-looking girl.

"Hi! Um, I'm—" she began, before the girl waved to someone behind her.

"Izz!" the girl called in a confident voice straight over Poppy's head. "Over here!"

"Hey, Daisy!"

Turning around, Poppy immediately recognised the girl from the tack shop, the one who'd bought her beautiful jacket. That's who the girl – Daisy – had been smiling at.

Izzy glanced at Poppy, then looked her up and down.

"Oh, I thought I'd seen you before," she said in a cool voice. "From Mandy's shop, right?"

Poppy glanced down at her jumper. The sequinned horseshoes seemed even more garish now.

"Yes," she said. "That's it. Hi."

"Yeah. Hi."

Poppy didn't know what else to say. Izzy hugged her friend and the two of them strolled off.

Feeling awkward, Poppy scuffed her jodhpur boots on the cobbles, wondering what to do.

"Hey!" A friendly voice interrupted her thoughts and to Poppy's relief a small girl bounded up, long black hair in a neat plait. "I'm Amina. Isn't this exciting?"

"Can't wait to find out which pony we're riding!" Another girl with a mass of curly black hair and a mischievous smile joined her on Poppy's other side. "Do you have any idea which pony you might be paired up with?"

"Hi! And no, not yet." Poppy hesitated. She didn't want to say yes, even though she knew in her heart she'd be paired with Silver Shadow!

"Sophieee, we'll find out soon enough." Amina grinned at the other girl. "Look, someone's coming. And she's got the list!"

As the parents gave their children a final hug goodbye, a smiling groom, trailed by a scruffy-looking spaniel, gathered all the camp members into the cool of the barn. As well as Sophie, Amina, Izzy from the tack shop and

Daisy, there were several other girls and a couple of boys, all clutching the camp booklet. Among them, a friendly-looking boy with sandy hair and freckles was buzzing around.

"Hey!" The boy joined Poppy, Amina and Sophie. "I'm Jack. Lainey's my mum," he explained. "I'm chuffed you're all here – might give me a break from the mucking out!" He was smiling as he said this, so Poppy grinned back.

"Emily!" Jack waved at a tall girl who was watching from the garden gate. She looked very like Jack, with the same sandy hair. "Come and say hi!"

Emily just scowled and folded her arms. Jack rolled his eyes.

"That's my sister. Ignore her," he said cheerfully. "She hates this bit, where everyone gets paired up with the ponies."

"Why?" Poppy asked curiously.

"Oh, Mum's been running these riding camps for a couple of years," Jack said. "Loads of kids come in the summer from town and Mum does other things too throughout the year, like pony-therapy camps. She's dead keen that *everyone* gets a chance to enjoy being around horses." He gestured around at the stables where all the gorgeous ponies were watching the new arrivals with interest. "But it means we've got to share. I don't mind." He grinned. "But Emily isn't so happy about other people riding and looking after them. Like I said," he added with a shrug, "just ignore her."

"OK, kids!" The groom clapped her hands and everyone turned to listen to her. "I'm Zoe. A big welcome to Vale Farm. Are you ready for a week of pony fun?"

Everyone cheered, and Zoe smiled.

"So we'll be doing plenty of riding, and there will be lots of fun and games too." She looked around at the group. "But most importantly, I want you to take complete care of the pony Lainey has partnered you with, as if he or she was your own. Get to know them, enjoy them. They've all got their own special personalities, just like you, and I'm certain Lainey has paired you with your perfect pony!"

Poppy held her breath as Zoe moved on to the bit everyone had been waiting for. It was time to find out who their pony was for the week! Lainey had asked all the camp members to fill in a form detailing their past riding experiences, as not all of the children rode at the stables regularly. Poppy thought back to her last ride, ages ago now, when she'd mastered a few strides of canter. And of course Lainey knew about her friendship with Silver Shadow because she had seen them together after school. She'd proudly put that on her form.

"Sophie, you're with Gorse. Amina, you've got Nutmeg." Zoe started to read from her list.

"Awesome!" Poppy heard Sophie say as she

headed out of the barn and made a beeline for a gorgeous bay pony across the yard.

Zoe moved down the list, and as she called out each child's name, they went out into the yard to meet their pony. There was Gracie and Bobby, a handsome piebald. Then Willow was paired with Luna, and Jess, a smiley girl with long dark hair, was matched with a pony called Merlin. So far everyone looked very happy with their pony partners!

Finally, only Poppy and Izzy were left. Poppy noticed that Izzy had on a T-shirt with her name – "Izz the Whizz" – and "Hardwick Manor Team Trials" above a logo of a jumping horse. *She'll definitely be good if she's been on a riding team,* Poppy thought.

"You two come with me," Zoe said. "Let's meet your ponies!"

Poppy's heart beat faster as she saw Silver

Shadow leaning over his stable door, his eyes seeming to search for her.

"OK, Izzy," Zoe said. "That's your pony, Misty, with the blue head collar on the hook."

Izzy flicked her ponytail over one shoulder and gave a cool smile. "Thanks, he's lovely. Hope he's a good jumper too."

"Oh, he's fantastic," Zoe replied. "He's a little buzzy, but Lainey will talk it all through with you."

Izzy nodded confidently, walking towards Silver Shadow's stable. Poppy felt the blood rush to her cheeks.

"Right then." Zoe smiled at Poppy, not seeming to notice her dismayed expression. "You've got dear old Henry. Come with me!" As Zoe marched ahead, Poppy watched Izzy pat the beautiful grey pony. *Her* dream pony.

Feeling the tears start to well up in her eyes, Poppy quickly blinked them away. Her throat felt thick and lumpy, and it was hard to swallow. Zoe was now opening the door to the last stable on the row, where a dark-bay pony greeted her with a gentle whicker.

For a moment, Poppy just stood and stared, her eyes moving from Henry's huge hairy hooves to the tips of his furry ears. He had a bristly mane that stood up straight like a hedgehog's prickles, and thick feathers on his solid legs. His head was a tiny bit too large for his body, but his eyes were soft and kind.

"This is Henry," Zoe said in an affectionate tone. "He's a real favourite of ours. He'll keep you safe."

As Zoe left to check on the other girls,

Poppy patted Henry, feeling his soft and velvety coat. He turned to investigate her pockets for treats, a hopeful look on his face.

She could hear the excited chatter of the other camp members as they hugged their ponies, calling out to each other about how lovely they were. And even worse, she could hear Izzy talking to Silver Shadow in the stable opposite.

"Well," Izzy said in a satisfied voice. "Aren't you beautiful?"

He was – Poppy knew that – but Silver Shadow wasn't just beautiful, he was her friend. For one moment she thought about phoning her mum and getting her to pick her up, not sure if she could bear watching someone else ride and care for *her* pony. Her dream of cantering the beautiful grey pony on the beach had been torn into a million pieces.

And as Henry nudged her, Poppy couldn't stop

the tears from spilling over as she leaned into him. This wasn't supposed to happen. Henry was lovely, but he wasn't Silver Shadow.

CHAPTER 3

"Right, everyone!"

Lainey strode into the yard, and Poppy hastily wiped her eyes as she peered out over the stable door.

"Let's start with a getting-to-know-your-pony session," Lainey continued. "They all love a good groom!"

There was a flurry of activity as head collars were fastened on and the ponies were led into the yard and tied to the rings outside each stable.

Poppy noticed Sophie's pony, a lovely bay with rich dapples, start to nibble at his lead rope, an innocent expression on his face as he pulled the rope loose. On the other side, Gracie was looking a little worried as her pony flattened his ears back and bobbed his head up and down. Poppy gave Henry's lead rope a gentle tug and with a loud groan the dark bay shuffled behind her out into the sunlight.

As Poppy brushed his coat with a rubber curry comb, Henry rested a leg and closed his eyes. Poppy looked over his back and across the yard to where Silver Shadow, or Misty as everyone else knew him, stood. Misty was tied up outside his stable, his head held high as he surveyed the comings and goings. Unlike Henry, whose bottom lip was now drooping heavily, Misty was almost buzzing with energy, the muscles rippling under his spotless white coat. Poppy wondered if he was looking for her as he danced around. She sighed, turning back to Henry and starting on the tangles in the pony's coarse mane.

"That's the wrong one," Poppy heard a voice say.

"That's the wrong brush for doing manes." Izzy stepped forward, sounding as if she was explaining the most obvious thing in the world. Poppy looked at the green rubber curry comb in her hand. She'd been so distracted by Misty that she'd forgotten to switch brushes.

"I know … I just…" But her words were drowned out by Izzy rooting noisily through Henry's grooming kit.

"You need something like this," Izzy instructed bossily, pulling out a round-headed brush quite similar to Poppy's own hairbrush. She ran it over the end section of Henry's mane and grimaced.

"Ugh," she said. "It's really tough, isn't it? Not like Misty's."

Poppy wanted to shout, to tell her she knew *exactly* what Misty's mane felt like, because she knew him way better than Izzy did. She knew how soft his curved ears were and how velvety his pink muzzle was, and how, up close, his grey flecks looked like stars. But instead she just nodded glumly. Part of her felt a bit bad for Henry. It wasn't his fault he had such a bristly mane and she knew she ought to stick up for him. But she'd been so looking forward to grooming her dream grey pony, and now Izzy had made her feel like a total beginner as well. Of course Poppy knew about grooming kits. She knew exactly which brush was used for what – she always scored top marks in the pony-magazine quizzes. She bit her lip, annoyed at herself.

"So, how long have you been riding?" Izzy asked.

Poppy shuffled her feet. She'd been dreading

this question. She'd loved ponies all her life, she'd read every single book the local library had to offer, and treasured every copy of *Pony* magazine, memorising the hints-and-tips page. But she didn't *actually* have that much riding experience.

"Oh, quite a long time. I had my first lesson when I was six," she said airily. Izzy didn't need to know that Poppy had only ridden once or twice a year since that first amazing birthday present.

"Well, *I've* been riding since before I could walk," said Izzy. "Lessons every week at Hardwick Manor. Have you heard of it?"

"Yes, of course," Poppy lied. She had no idea what Izzy was talking about, but she didn't want to let Izzy know that.

"So Lainey spoke to my instructor at Hardwick," Izzy continued breezily, "and she agreed I could ride Misty. Lainey knew *I'd* be OK with him. He's not a typical riding-school pony at all." With this, Izzy glanced at Henry, her lip curling just slightly as the bay pony shifted his weight, lifted his tail and let out an enormous fart, then gave a contented sigh as he resumed resting his leg.

Before Poppy could even think of a reply, Izzy had sauntered off. Poppy turned back to Henry's mane, this time using the right brush. It was going from bad to worse. Not only did she have to watch someone else with Silver Shadow, but that someone was Izzy. Taking her dream jacket was one thing, but her dream pony was quite another!

Poppy sniffed. She was grateful for Henry's sturdy neck that hid her face so that no one could see how upset she was. She wished Evie, her friend from school, was around. Amina and Sophie had been really nice, but without Silver Shadow to ride and care for, she felt so alone.

A few minutes later Lainey strolled by, just as Poppy was applying a slick of polish to Henry's big feet. Lainey paused, leaning on the stable door. She had lovely riding clothes on – neat breeches and brown boots, the sort that spoke of years and years in the saddle.

"Is everything OK, Poppy?" she asked gently, and Poppy straightened up, hanging her head. She didn't know how to tell Lainey why she was feeling so sad.

"I thought…" she said in a croaky voice. "I thought when I came here I'd ride Silver Shadow…" It all came out in a rush. "Because you knew how much I loved him."

Lainey looked a little confused for a second before she smiled kindly.

"Ah," she said. "Silver Shadow. Is that what you call Misty?"

"Yes," Poppy mumbled. "That's what he comes to when I call him."

"Well, he certainly likes you!" said Lainey "He

doesn't go to just anyone for a pat. And that name really suits him." Poppy felt a shiver of happiness. Lainey *had* noticed their bond. But then why had she paired her with another pony instead?

As if reading her thoughts, Lainey reached forward and patted Henry.

"But, Poppy," she said gently. "A pony on the ground can be very different to ride. Misty can be highly strung and does need a more experienced rider. I wanted you to have a good time at camp, which is why I thought Henry would be the perfect choice."

Poppy nodded, once again feeling a little guilty. Lainey must think she only wanted to ride Misty because he was flashier, but it wasn't that, although of course he was the most beautiful pony in the yard. It was because he was the pony who listened to all her chatter, let her plait his silken mane, nuzzled her gently when she'd had a bad day at

school. As Henry nudged her, she automatically patted him back, thinking about Lainey's words. She'd try and have the best week she could at camp, but it wasn't going to be the same.

CHAPTER 4

Once the ponies were groomed and the stables tidied, there was a break before lunch for the camp members to check out the barn they would be sleeping in and unpack their bags. Poppy's mum had been worried about it being draughty, but the barn walls were a warm honey-coloured stone, which made it feel surprisingly cosy.

For a few minutes the children milled around. The boys were in a little alcove at the end of the barn, and Sophie and Amina were chatting to some of the other girls Poppy recognised from the pony pairing. Feeling brave, she went and

joined them.

"We need to choose our beds. Bagsy this one!" Sophie grinned, making a leap for a camp bed. "Amina, Poppy, Gracie, Jess, Willow, over here!"

"Good one, Sophie." Amina hauled her bag over, dumping it on the next bed. "Let's stick together."

To Poppy's relief, Izzy and her friend Daisy, the girl Poppy had tried to say hello to earlier, were nowhere to be seen. She started to unpack, slowly pulling out her riding clothes but keeping them folded so as not to draw attention to them. She couldn't bear it if the other girls teased her about how bright they were.

But Gracie, the girl with the grumpy-looking piebald pony, turned to Poppy with a smile.

"I love your jodhs!" she exclaimed as Poppy looked at the bright-pink pair. "My mum wouldn't let me have anything fun." Gracie pulled out her own riding gear. "Boring old beige for me."

That had been exactly what Poppy wanted, but she smiled, feeling much better. She no longer felt as though she wanted to call her mum. Even though she didn't have her dream pony to ride, at least the other girls seemed really nice, and loved horses as much as she did!

"Is everyone pleased with their ponies?" Willow, cross-legged on her bed, threw her pillow at Sophie, who caught it with a chuckle.

"Couldn't be better," she replied. "Gorse is the best."

"Is he an Exmoor?" Poppy asked, thrilled she could use her pony-breed knowledge. She'd spent ages studying the native-breeds-of-Britain poster map on her bedroom wall.

"Yep," Sophie said. "And he's brilliant. So funny. He's already untied himself three times and knocked his water bucket over!"

"I've got Bobby," Gracie said with a little frown. "He's a bit grumpy … I hope he likes me soon."

"Luna's ace," Willow said. "She's meant to be super fast at games."

"No wonder Lainey partnered her with you," Gracie said. "Don't you run for the county?"

Willow nodded. "Yes," she replied. "I love them both – running and riding. Ponies more though."

"Always." Jess smiled. "What about Henry, Poppy?"

Poppy bit her lip. Truthfully, she'd been so busy thinking about Silver Shadow, or Misty, that she'd not really got to know Henry yet.

"He's err…" She struggled to think about how to describe Henry. "He's nice."

Jess looked at her thoughtfully, her dark eyes full of questions, and Poppy wondered if she'd picked up on her uncertain tone. Then Jess changed the subject.

"I wonder how 'Izz the Whizz' will get on with Misty?" she said. "He's meant to be a bit of a handful."

"I'd rather stick with Gorse," Sophie said. "I want to have fun, thanks!"

"Misty is the most beautiful, gentle pony ever," Poppy blurted out, and everyone turned to look at her. She felt herself blush but she had to stick up for Misty. Once again, a little voice questioned why she hadn't stood up for Henry earlier when Izzy had been so mean about his mane.

"Do you know him?" Jess asked.

Poppy nodded. "I see him every day," she explained. "I visit him after school. I love him so much, I…" And to her awful embarrassment, hot tears started to fall. She was upset, but she was annoyed too. Annoyed Izzy had got to ride Misty instead of her, and annoyed she had corrected her about the grooming kits.

"Hey!" Amina was beside her in a flash. "Don't be upset! Camp is meant to be fun." She gave Poppy's shoulders a squeeze.

"Did you think Misty was going to be your pony?" Jess said gently.

Poppy nodded. "Yes," she said, wiping her eyes. "Lainey always saw me with him. I thought she'd noticed how well we got on together."

Willow tilted her head to one side. "But there's more to it than that, isn't there?" She shrugged. "If you're not experienced enough for him, then that'll be the reason."

Poppy knew Willow was right, but she couldn't help but feel the sting of her words.

Willow, as if realising she'd been a little harsh, smiled. "But I'm sure Henry's great. All Lainey's ponies are lovely," she said kindly.

"It'll work out!" Sophie threw her pillow at Poppy. "You'll still have a brilliant week with Henry! Come on, let's go for lunch. We've got the riding to look forward to later!"

Feeling more cheerful, Poppy headed out with her new friends to a trestle table set up under the big oak tree at the far end of the yard. The sheep she'd seen earlier, who Poppy had learned was called Mini, was waiting hopefully next to the

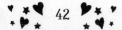

table. Every now and again she was shooed away by a kind-looking lady who was putting a paper bag on each plate. Smiling, she beckoned them over.

"Just a minute, kids! Have a sit down in the shade!"

Doing as they were told, the girls flopped down underneath the tree, enjoying the cool shade of its branches as Mini rustled and nosed among them.

Willow frowned, wriggling a bit as though she had sat on something.

"What's this?" She moved over and, where the glint of something metal could just be seen, cleared away the dusty earth with her hands. Everyone gathered round, looking at the object she picked up. A horseshoe! Poppy peered at it. The metal was soft and worn and there was a faint inscription in the curve of the shoe.

"I can't quite read it," she said, squinting at the words. "I wonder where it's from?"

"Well, wherever it's from, I reckon it's a sign! Horseshoes are meant to be lucky, aren't they?" Amina grinned.

"We'll hang it above our camp beds!" Sophie grinned. "Let's do it now while we're waiting!"

Everyone agreed this was a great idea, all jumping up in a rush of giggles and chatter to follow Sophie back to the barn. Poppy felt a ripple of happiness, no longer missing Evie so much. Now she'd made some new friends, the week was definitely looking up – even more so when, as the tallest in the group, she was the one who got to hang the horseshoe up. All the girls clapped as the horseshoe caught a beam of light, making the dull metal sparkle.

"To the best camp ever!" said Amina.

Just as in the barn, Sophie took charge once

lunch was all set up, pulling out the benches so the six girls could sit together at the end of the table. Izzy and Daisy were at the far end, deep in conversation, with the two boys sitting in the middle.

"Come on!" Sophie gestured to the seats. "Let's stick together!"

Starving hungry, Poppy opened her lunch bag.

The sandwiches looked delicious – big chunks of bread with cheese and pickle, a shiny red apple and a homemade cookie. Misty was in his stable on the other side of the yard, watching the lunch with interest, but Poppy felt sure he was watching her most of all. Automatically her eyes moved to Henry's stable where the little pony was snoozing in the shade. Poppy could only see the tops of his ears and the fluff of his forelock sticking up above the door. It looked so sweet that it brought a smile to her face. Misty might be her dream pony but Henry was hers for the week.

Ever since she'd chatted with the rest of the girls, a plan had been forming in Poppy's mind. If she impressed Lainey with Henry this week, then perhaps she could ride Misty eventually, even if it wasn't until camp next year. Perhaps she could ask her mum and dad for a couple more riding lessons for birthday and Christmas presents so she'd be more experienced. And maybe she could see if her neighbours' cars needed washing, or their dogs needed walking. That way she could earn enough to pay for her own lessons. Somehow she'd find a way to ride Misty.

She finished the last of her lunch, excited about the riding that afternoon now she had a plan. She was going to get good enough to ride her Silver Shadow!

CHAPTER 5

When Poppy went to tack him up a bit later, Henry was flat out on his side, fast asleep.

"Henry!" Poppy clicked her tongue. Henry opened one eye and briefly lifted his head before giving a deep sigh, laying his head back down and shutting his eye again.

"Henry?" Poppy repeated, crouching beside him and giving his shoulder a gentle nudge. "It's time to ride."

Was Henry actually snoring?

"Come on, boy." Poppy bit her lip, unsure what to do. "Let's try your head collar." With a little difficulty, as Henry's head was surprisingly heavy, Poppy managed to fasten the head collar on. Tugging gently at the rope, Poppy tried to encourage the little pony to get up, but he gave another loud groan.

She felt panic rising in her stomach. Something wasn't right. Henry wasn't even opening his eyes now, just making the same ominous groaning noises. Kneeling down again, Poppy placed an ear to his tummy and felt her heart stop as it gave a gurgling rumble. Henry must be ill. Her mind raced back to her pony books. Henry was

groaning and reluctant to get up. It could only be one thing, the thing every horse person feared. Colic. She needed to find Lainey, and fast!

Poppy quickly unfastened the head collar with shaking fingers, giving Henry a hug.

"I'll get you help, boy. Hold on!" she called, letting herself out of the stable before running smack bang into Izzy.

"What's up?" Izzy asked, and Poppy gestured to the stable, hardly able to speak as she choked back a sob.

"It's Henry," she stammered. "He's ill!"

Izzy glanced into the stable. "What are you talking about?" She shrugged dismissively. "He's just asleep."

A bubble of anger rose in Poppy. She knew Henry was ill. Izzy might have been right about the brushes but she wasn't right this time!

"He's got colic!" she cried. "I read about it in

my stable-management book. It's obvious!"

And without waiting for an answer, Poppy sprinted as fast as she could towards Lainey.

"Lainey!" Poppy yelled, aware everyone was now looking at her. "It's Henry!" Her voice was high with panic, her breath coming out in short gasps. "Please help!"

Lainey followed Poppy as she rushed back to Henry's stable, her heart pounding. What if it was too late? Why hadn't she gone to say hello to him straight after her lunch instead of staying to chat to Amina and looking through *Pony* magazine? She would have found him before he lay down, unable to get up again.

"See!" Poppy peered over the door, where Henry was still flat out on his side. And – oh no! – his groans were getting louder now. They'd need to get the emergency vet. This was serious.

But to her surprise, Lainey chuckled!

"Ah," Lainey said. "There's something I forgot to tell you about Henry…"

Letting herself into the stable, Lainey gave Henry's generous hindquarters a pat.

"Come on, old boy," she said affectionately. She made a sort of chrrr, chrrr sound. "Time to get up, sleepy head!"

To Poppy's amazement, Henry stopped groaning, lifted his head and looked crossly at Lainey.

"He's always done this." Lainey laughed as Henry clambered slowly to his feet and stretched luxuriously before shaking himself, shavings flying off his dark-brown coat like snow. His mane was sticking up and he had an enormous stable stain down the side of his tummy from where he had lain in poo. Bright-eyed, the little pony nudged Lainey.

"He pretends he can't hear you," Lainey

explained, giving him a hug. "He knows he can't get away with it with me, so I expect he thought he'd try it on with you!"

"Oh." Poppy slumped with relief. "But what about his tummy? It was rumbling really loudly, and he was making all those groaning noises. Like he was in pain!"

There was a stifled giggle from outside the stable and, looking up, Poppy flushed as she saw Izzy laughing with Daisy, obviously listening to every word. Lainey glanced at them and gave a little frown.

"I'm really pleased you're so observant," she said kindly but louder, as if making sure Izzy and Daisy could really hear her. "And you're right, it could have been that Henry was seriously ill from what you saw of him lying down. But actually a rumbly tummy is perfectly healthy, and some are just rumblier than others. And the groaning noises ... well, that's just Henry. He's got quite a sense of humour. I've had to wake him up for every single afternoon lesson since he arrived here ten years ago!"

Henry looked sideways at Poppy. It was almost as though he was smiling. *So Izzy was right again*, Poppy thought in dismay.

"There's no time to groom," Lainey continued, flicking a few shavings off with her hands. "Don't worry about the stable stain, we'll sort that later." She paused and smiled at Poppy. "And well done for coming to find me. That was the right thing to do – never ignore your instincts."

Poppy nodded, feeling a mixture of relief and pride at Lainey's words, and a growing sense of embarrassment. Izzy and Daisy had scurried off, no longer laughing, which made her feel slightly better, but she still felt really silly.

She wished she could spend a bit of time

smoothing out Henry's mane but they were running late. Soon he was all tacked up and being led out to join the others, who were waiting for them in the outdoor arena. In the line-up of ponies, there was only one that Poppy really saw – her beautiful Misty, his coat sparkling white, his mane perfect. Izzy was wearing a gorgeous pair of soft sand-coloured breeches and long chestnut-leather boots. Poppy's cheeks grew hot as she looked down at the bright-pink jodhpurs. Gracie might like them but she didn't. They'd do while she rode Henry but when she was good enough to ride Misty, she was going to dress just like Izzy.

❤

"Up down, up down. Good!" Lainey called from the centre of the arena as Poppy completed her solo lap of the school. Henry's trot was bouncy but she felt surprisingly secure in the saddle, his bristly mane and neck solid in front of her, the plaited reins cool in her hands. Henry never went faster or slower than required. But as Poppy glanced in the mirror she saw that, despite her best efforts, Henry's neck stuck out, his muzzle held low. It hardly looked elegant – there was no outline at all. In her books, it said you needed to use your seat and legs to encourage the pony to work into an outline rather than use your hands to force it to arch its neck.

But Henry just trotted around and Poppy felt he would probably do exactly the same whatever

she tried to do. Instead she concentrated on her position, feeling sure Henry wouldn't try to take off or buck or anything else she'd been worried about. She wanted to be able to canter on him perfectly for the beach ride in just two days' time.

By contrast, Misty looked magical. His neck was beautifully rounded into the perfect outline and Izzy's hands were soft on the reins. It was as though she was hardly moving in the saddle as she asked the grey to canter, which he did with a powerful leap forward. As he danced around the school, Poppy imagined that riding him was probably the best feeling in the world. She nudged Henry into a safe but lumbering canter at last, holding on to a handful of bristly mane as well as her reins, and sighed. She couldn't wait to find out for herself just what it was like to ride that beautiful grey pony.

A big part of camp was pony care. After supper, Poppy refilled Henry's water bucket before cleaning out his stable and stuffing his hay net. Although one of the main reasons she'd opted to stay at camp was so that she could just hang out with Misty in the evenings, she found herself chatting away to Henry. Henry seemed to listen, a serious expression on his face as she recounted her day.

But it didn't feel right to tell Henry about her plan to become a better rider on him so she could ride Misty! Despite his earlier performance in the stable, Poppy was very grateful to Henry for behaving nicely in the lesson. Letting herself out of Henry's stable, she smiled as Misty whickered at her. Izzy wasn't around so, crossing the yard, Poppy hugged him, breathing in the lemony-fly-spray-mixed-with-horse smell, feeling his coat silken and cool against her cheek.

"Good night. I love you so much," she whispered. "And I've got a plan."

It was OK to tell Misty now Henry was out of earshot. She reached up to stroke his forelock. "You see, what I'm going to do is to make sure I can ride you one day – very soon too." She gave him one last hug, finally tearing herself away. But as she started to head back to the barn where her new friends were waiting for her to play rounders, she heard a throaty whicker and turned to see Henry peering at her over his stable door, his head bobbing up and down. Quickly running back, she planted a kiss on his muzzle, laughing as his bristly chin tickled her.

"And good night to you."

Misty might be her dream pony, but Henry was very sweet too!

CHAPTER 6

Everyone was excited about the jumping lesson
the next morning. The children were going to be
taught by Jade, Vale Farm's riding instructor. She
kept her horse, a beautiful grey showjumper, at
the yard. Poppy knew Jade had started out as a
Saturday helper at the stables, and Poppy hoped
to impress her in the jumping lessons. She made
sure she was in the yard early to give herself time
to smarten Henry up, and after brushing his
dark-brown coat, applying hoof polish and using
a special spray on his mane, her hard work paid
off. Henry looked lovely, and he'd really enjoyed

the extra pampering too. Poppy still longed to be brushing the silken white of Misty's coat but it had been really rewarding giving Henry a special makeover. And it was even better when Jade complimented her.

"Wow, Henry!" Jade said. "You look ever so smart. Well done, Poppy."

But even though Henry looked smart, it didn't give him any extra oomph in his jumping lesson.

"Come on, Henry!" Jade called in an encouraging voice as Poppy had her turn over the little course. "See if you can canter on, Poppy."

But despite Poppy's best efforts, Henry barely broke out of a trot and hardly jumped the first cross-pole, merely lifting his legs a little higher. Poppy couldn't help but feel deflated, especially as Misty and Izzy had soared gracefully over everything. She needed to show Jade what she could do so Jade could tell Lainey, Poppy thought.

This was so important.

Determinedly, she gave Henry an extra nudge with her heels as they turned down to a straight bar. Leaning over the saddle, she tried to urge him on, moving her hands around to try to encourage him. But to her horror, Henry just got slower and slower until he came to a complete stop, thrusting his big head downwards and nudging at the pole with his muzzle. Totally unbalanced and unable to stop herself, Poppy did a complete somersault over his neck in awful slow motion. As the rest of the class broke into giggles, she found herself sitting on the sand with Henry gazing down at her, tickling her cheek with his bristly whiskers.

Jade came over to Poppy and gave her a hand up. "All OK?" she asked, looking concerned.

Poppy nodded. She wasn't hurt, just embarrassed. "Yes," she mumbled. "Why did he do that?"

Jade smiled. "I know you didn't mean to but when you moved your hands around like that, you pulled at his mouth," she said in the same kind tone Lainey had used the day before when Poppy had been convinced Henry had colic. "You were urging him on and pulling back all at the same time, so he took matters into his own hands, or hooves, really. When it comes to jumping Henry, you just need to let him be."

"What do you mean?" Poppy said miserably, wiping sand from the bright-pink jodhpurs.

"I mean just that," Jade explained. "Henry might not be the most stylish but he's safe, so you can concentrate on your jumping position. He doesn't like being hurried or told what to do. He knows what to do. Here, have another go." And she legged Poppy up into the saddle before Poppy could think about it.

Poppy took a deep breath and turned Henry back down to a little cross-pole. She didn't want to embarrass herself again, especially as she was sure she'd seen Izzy smirk. This time she left Henry's mouth well alone, just as Jade had said. She simply concentrated on sitting up straight before folding neatly as Henry, ears pricked, leapt over the poles in a surprisingly nimble fashion. And as Poppy landed, she couldn't help but grin. That was more like it!

As Poppy went back into line after a few more successful jumps, Sophie leaned over with a smile. "See! Told you you'd have a brilliant time with Henry."

Poppy smiled back.

"I am," she said. And it was totally true! She had barely thought about Misty while she was jumping.

Jade called all the riders around her.

"I think it's time for some fun and games," she said. "What do you all say to some gymkhana races?"

Everyone whooped, apart from Izzy and her friend Daisy, who just wrinkled their noses a bit.

Jack, who'd been sitting on the fence watching, leapt down and joined the group. "Jade, can I set up the games?"

Jade nodded. "Go on then," she said. "Let's think of some good ones."

Poppy tried to listen carefully as Jade and Jack explained the rules of each game and divided the group into two teams. She smiled at Gracie and Willow as Jade pointed for her to join their side, but her tummy flipped over as Jade sent Izzy to their team too. She glanced around her. Everyone looked as though they knew what they were doing. But Poppy had never taken part in a gymkhana. And then there was the added pressure of trying to make Henry canter!

Waiting her turn on the first relay race, Poppy hoped she wouldn't make a fool of herself as she nudged Henry and grabbed a baton from a laughing Gracie. She had to ride round the barrels that had been set up in a line, moving a cup from one barrel to the next before handing the baton to the next rider in the team.

"Come on, Henry!" Gracie called, slowing Bobby down as Poppy urged Henry on.

But as Henry steered in and out of the barrels, Poppy relaxed, realising he was actually really good at games! He seemed to be helping her, getting as close as possible to the barrel when she had to pick up the cup, turning his body so he was at exactly the right angle before leaping forward as if determined to win.

The next game was a simple bending race and Henry showed a surprising turn of speed. When it came to the race where each rider had to carry a cup of water from one side of the arena to the other, he seemed to trot extra carefully as Poppy held the full cup without spilling a drop.

In the next race, Poppy had to dismount after trotting to a pole and run back as fast as she could, getting Henry to follow her as she clutched a treat in her hand. Ears pricked, his big heavy hooves scuffing up the sand as he trotted behind her, Henry gobbled up the treat at the finish line, a look of delight on his face. Rosy-cheeked and laughing, Poppy gave him a huge hug. She hadn't thought Henry was really capable of such speed – maybe he would actually be able to keep up with the others on the beach ride!

"Awesome!" Willow cheered. "You've just won us that race. I reckon we can win the whole thing!"

"A draw so far." Jade clapped her hands. "It all depends on this last race. Ride up, swap ponies, ride back. Fastest team wins!"

Poppy held her breath as Jade quickly organised the riders into pairs. With growing excitement, Poppy realised the pony she was going to swap to was Misty. It might only be a quick canter back through some poles, but it didn't matter. The fun of riding Henry in the games was nothing compared to this, and any achievement from the jumping session was quickly forgotten. Finally she'd ride her dream pony, her Silver Shadow!

CHAPTER 7

Everyone was in high spirits but Izzy didn't look happy about the pony swap. Reaching the end of the arena, Poppy leapt off Henry in one swift movement, ready to hand her reins to Izzy, who dismounted much more slowly with an eye roll. Poppy could hardly believe it was happening as she swung herself into Misty's saddle. She'd grown used to Henry, so sturdy and wide. For a split second she found herself missing the lovely feeling of safety Henry gave her, with his broad back and solid neck. But she shook that thought away. Riding Misty was everything she had dreamed of, after all!

"Well, we'd better at least try to win." Izzy grimaced and gave Henry a hard nudge. "Oh my goodness, he's so ploddy and fat!"

Poppy frowned. She knew Henry wouldn't like being nudged like that, and it wasn't kind to say he was ploddy!

"He's not! You don't need to—" But her words were lost as Izzy pushed Henry into a lumbering canter, as if she wanted to get her ride on him over and done with as quickly as possible. Following close behind, Misty also broke into a canter and it was as though he was flying, his feet barely seeming to touch the ground. Despite feeling bad for Henry, Poppy couldn't help but laugh out loud. Riding Misty was even better than she'd imagined.

But as they neared the finish line, Henry slowed up and trotted straight into their path, heading for the open bag of treats Jade had left on the side. Izzy looked furious, trying to steer him back to the finish line. They weren't close to Poppy and Misty, but to Poppy's horror Misty veered and spooked. Poppy had to use all her strength to stay on, her feet flying out of their stirrups as she grasped a handful of Misty's silky mane. Red faced, she wriggled back into the saddle in an undignified manner and managed to finally cross the finish line.

Poppy felt a stab of disappointment. Not only had they just lost the race, meaning the other team had won overall, but that had been her chance to show Lainey and Jade how well she could ride Misty and she'd almost fallen off! She slid down the saddle and hugged him tight as he nestled into her, exactly as he did when she visited him in his field.

"He's never done that with me!" Izzy called as she rode over. "He obviously knew he had a novice on his back."

Poppy glared at her. It wasn't Misty's fault – after all, Izzy had let Henry cross their path. She looked at Henry, who was still gazing longingly at the treats, and felt cross with him. Izzy might have lost control but it was greedy Henry who had caused the spook. She gave Misty a pat.

"I will get better," Poppy whispered to him. "And I'll ride you again, I promise."

She looked up. Izzy was now laughing with Daisy.

"Bet you didn't think you'd have to ride him!" Daisy grimaced.

"Oh, don't." Izzy scowled, thrusting Henry's reins back to Poppy. "Thank goodness Lainey paired me with Misty."

Poppy looked at Henry, at his big, soft eyes, and any feelings of irritation quickly disappeared. Poor sweet Henry! It was a good thing he couldn't understand what the girls were saying. Giving Misty a final pat, Poppy took Henry's reins and gave him a big hug.

"You did brilliantly, boy," she said loudly, hoping Izzy and Daisy would feel guilty for being so mean. She had been mean too, she thought, feeling guilty herself. "You helped us win the treat race!"

Lainey came over, a smile on her face.

"Wow!" she said to Poppy. "You rode Misty really nicely there. You did well keeping him calm after the spook and that was a lovely canter. Henry is teaching you well."

Poppy felt a bubble of happiness grow.

"Actually, I've been meaning to talk to you," Lainey continued thoughtfully as everyone headed back to the stables. "Your concern for Henry yesterday, and your brilliant stable management have really made me think. I've got a Saturday space free – it'll be a morning helping on the yard, in exchange for a lesson. I wondered if you'd like to take the place?"

"Oh, wow!" Poppy gasped. "Yes, please. I'd love that."

"I'll talk to your mum," Lainey said with a smile. "Then you've got some pony time to look forward to after camp."

Once Lainey had gone, Poppy looked over at

Misty, her beautiful Misty. If she was going to be at Vale Farm each week, surely this meant she might have a chance to ride him more regularly? Her plan was working. But as Henry ambled back to his stable, ears pricked, a merry swing to his walk, she automatically placed an arm around his neck. Misty was her dream, but Henry was the one helping her achieve it!

"Wakey-wakey, sleepyhead!"

Sophie nudged Poppy, who groaned and reached for her watch. She had been certain she was going to wake up before her alarm, but all the riding and fresh air had made her super tired! Blearily she sat up in her camp bed and looked outside where the first rays of sunshine were creeping up over the paddocks, catching the horseshoe, making it sparkle in the early morning light.

"The beach ride, remember?" Sophie grinned.

But Poppy had already leapt out of bed. The beach ride was the thing she had been most looking forward to!

"How could I forget!" she said, pulling on her jodhpurs and a T-shirt. "Race you out to the stables!"

There was a deep, rumbly whinny from Misty as Poppy and Sophie and the rest of the girls ran into the yard.

"Hello, sweetheart," Poppy called out as she crossed over the cobbles. She jumped as an even louder whinny sounded, and looking up she saw Henry, his big head bobbing up and down. He whinnied again hopefully. Suddenly Poppy was torn, but she was nearer Misty so gave him a hug first, pressing her nose into his silken neck. She knew she was imagining it, but it seemed to her that there was hurt in Henry's lovely soft eyes as he gazed at her before turning back to his hay net.

"I'll be back in a minute." Poppy finally tore herself away from Misty and went to Henry, clicking with her tongue to entice him back over the stable door. He didn't need much encouragement and was soon nudging his soft nose into Poppy's arm. Lainey emerged from her house carrying a mug of coffee.

"Oh, how lovely!" she said. "Henry loves all the attention he gets during camp."

Poppy felt horribly guilty all of a sudden. Henry was so sweet, and she bet all of his other riders made a big fuss of him all the time. She needed to do the same.

CHAPTER 8

"Right then, listen everyone!"

Lainey halted her horse at the riding-school gates and turned to face the camp members as they lined up on their ponies. The ponies seemed to know that they were off somewhere exciting and a few jigged about a bit, especially Misty, but Henry just gave a deep sigh and rested a leg.

"That's Major Green!" Jess whispered to Poppy in an awestruck voice. She gestured towards Lainey's lovely horse, a chestnut with a white splodge on his neck. "But everyone knows him as Bertie. Lainey won Badminton on him! He's about twenty now."

"That's really cool." Poppy grinned. Not only was she about to head off on the breakfast beach ride, but a famous horse was going along with them! In just a short space of time, she had ridden Silver Shadow and now she was going to ride alongside a Badminton winner. Best week ever!

"We're heading out past the golf course and on to the heathland," Lainey explained. "And then down to the beach. They all know the route well, so relax and enjoy it!"

There was an excited murmur among the group, and Poppy and her new friends grinned at each other.

"The ponies know exactly what to do," Lainey said. "If you follow me in a line, there's nowhere for them to go, and then we'll all wait at the groynes at the end. But if one of you doesn't want to canter, we'll all stick to a trot. Not a problem at

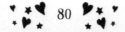

all. So all those who want to canter on the beach, put your hands up!"

Everyone, including Poppy, stuck their hand up. Although Poppy was the rider with the least experience, she knew Henry would look after her. And she felt so much more confident after the last few days! But as they clip-clopped down the quiet lanes leading away from town, she had to work hard to make sure they kept up with the rest of the gang.

"Are you OK?" Amina called back to her, and Poppy nodded, wishing Henry could go just a bit faster. At this rate she wouldn't get the thrill of a canter along the golden sand! "Come on, boy." She squeezed with her legs but there was no change in Henry's speed, even as they snaked down the dusty path through the heathland and over the sand dunes to the beach that stretched before them, the sea blue and sparkling in the sun.

"Are you still happy to canter?" Lainey called, and a resounding "Yes" came back from the group. "Then follow me, and no overtaking!" Lainey instructed, and she nudged Bertie into a beautiful collected canter. One by one the ponies followed steadily, their riders grinning as they splashed in and out of the shallows. But try as she might, there was no way Poppy could get Henry to canter. He just stuck to the same steady trot, barely seeming to notice as the waves lapped around his hooves.

Amina turned around again. "We'll wait for

you at the end!" she called as Nutmeg cantered on, past Izzy and Misty, to join the rest of the group.

Poppy gazed enviously at Misty, thinking how magical it must feel for Izzy. Then she frowned. Something wasn't right. A big black dog raced across the sand chasing a tennis ball, suddenly swerving towards Misty who spooked dramatically, spinning around like a whirlwind. Izzy was thrown sideways and had to cling on. Then Misty was galloping back the way they had come, and, with the rest of the group far ahead, Poppy realised that only she and Henry knew what was going on.

"Misty, please steady!" Izzy sounded desperate as Misty tore past Henry, who gave a snort of surprise.

Poppy felt as if her heart had stopped. She knew there was no way she'd be able to catch up with the others to let them know what had happened.

And Misty, her beautiful Misty, had galloped off! She had to go after him.

"Come on, boy!" Poppy turned Henry around and, as if he knew what she wanted, he broke into a determined canter. Even speedier than he had been in the bending race, he followed Misty back up the beach and towards the dunes. Poppy crouched over Henry's neck, urging him to keep going as they chased Misty and Izzy along the path.

"Izzy!" she called. "Hold on!"

Misty was slowing a bit and Poppy began to catch up.

"Nearly there!" she cried. "Good boy, Henry."

But Misty snorted and made a sharp turn as the dunes got steeper and the path narrower. Izzy went flying through the air, tumbling over on the sun-bleached marram grass. Misty slowed to a halt as Izzy sat up with a cry, clutching her foot.

"My ankle!"

Poppy leapt off Henry and quickly put the reins over his head, just the way she remembered from her pony-care books, and led him while she ran to Izzy.

"Izzy!" she said, crouching down next to her. "Are you OK?"

Izzy winced and stretched her ankle a bit.

"I don't think it's broken," she said shakily. "But it really hurts."

"It's probably sprained." Poppy looked around her in concern. There was no sign of the other riders and Misty was loose. Although he had stopped, Poppy knew that if he broke into a gallop again and carried on to going the same way, he would head straight on to the main road. She had to catch him. It was time to use their special connection, their bond.

CHAPTER 9

"Come on, boy!"

Handing Henry's reins to Izzy, Poppy took a deep breath, thinking about the way she would call for the grey after school and how he would always canter over to her. "Silver Shadow! It's me, Poppy."

Poppy was aware of Izzy giving her a funny look.

"Silver Shadow?" she said, one eyebrow raised. "His name's Misty."

"I know," Poppy said through gritted teeth. "Come on, boy," she called to Misty again. "Let's get you home."

All those afternoons spent chatting to him, building up the trust between them, were now going to pay off, and she could show Izzy that she was just as good with Misty. His ears were pricked as he looked towards her. Edging forward, Poppy reached up to grab the trailing reins that had been thrown over Misty's head when Izzy tumbled off. But as she closed her hand round them, Misty leapt into the air, knocking her over. She ended up sitting heavily on the ground, winded, with

Misty standing a couple of metres away, quivering with nerves and energy, and staring ahead in the direction of the main road. He looked as though he was going to make a run for it.

But then Henry, his reins still held by Izzy, made a soft whickering sound, and Misty answered, glancing towards his stable mate. Something suddenly struck Poppy. "Henry!" she said out loud, heading back to the dark bay. "Misty doesn't want to leave Henry!"

Henry nudged her hard, as though he'd been trying to tell her all along.

"OK, Henry, let's try something together."

Putting the reins over his head and hopping back into the saddle, Poppy nudged him forward, walking over to Misty. She talked softly to the grey, who was still on high alert, his head aloft, his dark eyes searching for something in the distance. He let out a trembling whinny but stayed still.

"Come on," she said softly. "Look, Henry's here."

Poppy had watched old cowboy films in which riders swung out of their saddles to catch loose horses. It looked so easy when they did it. But in reality, she knew leaning over to catch the loose reins would be much harder. It would be wobbly and unsafe and she really didn't want to fall off. As well as potentially hurting herself badly, she didn't want to spook Misty even further.

But as they drew alongside Misty, Poppy realised that Henry had placed himself perfectly, just as he had done in the gymkhana races. He stood square, solid and unmoving as Poppy leaned out of her saddle as far as she dared and made a grab for the reins. She had him! Misty gave a startled lurch and for a split second Poppy was almost dragged off her own saddle. But Henry swiftly took a few steps back, mirroring Misty, who came to a stop, his sides heaving. His reins were still in Poppy's hands and he was safe.

Misty nuzzled Henry's big soft nose before the dark bay gave him a gentle nip on the neck, as if telling him off.

Shakily, Poppy nudged Henry on so he walked back to Izzy, and Misty followed quietly alongside him.

"Izzy," she said slowly. "Did you see that?"

And Izzy nodded. "You and Henry worked together!" she said, her eyes wide. "You're the perfect team!"

Izzy managed to get herself up, standing unsteadily on her sore ankle. Sliding down from Henry's saddle, Poppy gave both ponies a pat.

"Shall I give you a leg up on to Misty?" Poppy asked.

Izzy paused. "Actually," she said in a shaky voice. "Can I ride Henry?"

Henry nudged Poppy and she felt his solid, reassuring presence. He deserved a whole bucket of carrots when they got back!

"OK," Poppy agreed. "I'll help you on. Let's go and find the rest of the group."

It wasn't quite as she'd imagined, but she was going to ride Misty, the pony of her dreams, along the beach. She didn't feel the same rush of excitement she'd felt before she rode him during the gymkhana games.

Misty seemed completely calm again and so she climbed up into his saddle, giving him a pat.

"Thanks so much for coming after me," Izzy said in a quiet voice, sitting safely on Henry. "Imagine if Misty had got on the road…" She shuddered, her voice trailing off.

"I had to check Misty was OK," Poppy said simply. "And you, of course," she added. Izzy had been mean about Henry, but she had needed Poppy's help.

"But Henry is the one we both need to thank," she continued, looking down at the dark bay.

"I know," Izzy agreed. "I'm sorry I was so horrible about him. He's an amazing pony."

Reaching forward, Izzy gave Henry a hug, and Poppy wished she could do the same, and say sorry too. Sorry for being ashamed of his sticking-up mane and his big heavy head. Sorry that she'd been annoyed when she had fallen off in the jumping lesson, and when Henry had refused to canter on the beach. Sorry that she'd only seen him as a stepping stone to Misty, when really he was perfect in his very own way.

As they walked down the path back on to the beach, a shout interrupted Poppy's thoughts and Lainey appeared on her horse, her face tight with worry. The other riders were behind her.

"Oh, thank goodness!" she cried. "Are you OK? What happened?"

Poppy looked at Henry, so wise and kind.

Reaching over and patting Henry's neck, Poppy grinned at Lainey.

"Henry saved the day!"

CHAPTER 10

"I always knew he was a special pony," Lainey said a little later, after Poppy and Izzy had recounted their story. They were back in the yard and sitting outside Henry's stable, where the little dark bay was eating his breakfast after a well-deserved roll. "He's a hero!"

"He really is." Poppy nodded. She'd given Henry the biggest hug and his promised carrots. She'd hugged Misty too. It hadn't really been his fault – he was a spooky pony and the dog had obviously scared him. *My books were right*, Poppy thought. *Horses are unpredictable*.

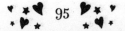

"It must have been really scary!" Gracie said as Poppy sat down for breakfast.

"It was a bit," Poppy said truthfully. "But I knew Henry would look after me, once I realised I needed his help."

"And you got to ride Misty on the beach, just like you wanted!" Jess smiled.

"I did," Poppy said. And she had! But something hadn't felt right. She'd missed

Henry's bristly mane, that solid, dependable neck, those sweet furry ears.

Sophie sat down next to the girls and nudged Poppy.

"I heard from Daisy that Izzy's going home to let her ankle rest," she said. "Lainey said she can join camp next week or the week after instead, so that's OK. But that means Misty will be free!" She gave a big grin. "And I overheard Lainey saying she was going to ask if you want to ride him!"

For a second, Poppy felt her heart stop. Misty, her Silver Shadow. But then a little movement caught her eye and she saw Henry's big kind face reaching over his stable door, intent on snatching a mouthful of hay from the bale Zoe was wheeling past in a barrow. She chuckled. Typical sweet greedy Henry.

"Poppy?" Lainey said in a quiet voice, once

everyone had cleared up after breakfast. "Have you got a minute?"

Her tummy fluttering, Poppy followed Lainey over to the cool of the barn.

"I'm sure you've heard by now that Izzy is going to miss the rest of camp as her ankle gets better," Lainey explained. "Would you like to ride Misty a bit more this week? I know how much you love him. We won't be doing any more beach riding, but you can certainly ride him in the arena..."

Poppy took a deep breath. Her head was spinning. She did love Misty so, so much. But there was another pony she had grown to love. A pony who'd shown her that pony books don't teach you everything. A pony who had exasperated and embarrassed her, but then shown her what a hero looked like too. Her mind was made up.

"Actually," she said. "I think I'll stick with Henry."

Lainey smiled.

"Of course," she said kindly. "Henry is a star. And perhaps you could pamper Misty a bit now he doesn't have a rider? He'd love a good groom, and I know you two have a wonderful relationship. I'm sure he'll enjoy a few days out in the field instead of at camp."

Poppy nodded. "I'd love that."

Now that she could hang out with her two favourite ponies, camp was going to be twice as much fun!

But there was one more thing she needed to ask.

"And can I ride Henry in my lessons, when I come for my Saturday job?"

"Absolutely!" Lainey chuckled. "I think you and Henry are good friends now, don't you?"

Emerging back into the sunshine, Poppy headed straight for Henry's stable and gave him a hug, before doing the same to Misty. Going back to Henry, she placed her forehead against his big generous forehead, and laughed as his bristly forelock tickled her cheek. Two ponies, so different, but both so special.

And she knew now that when she rushed to the fields after school, there were two ponies she was going to call for. One, her Silver Shadow, the pony who cantered through her dreams. And the other, kind and loyal Henry, the pony who had cantered straight into her heart.

ARE YOU A PERFECT PONY PRO? TAKE THIS QUIZ TO FIND OUT!

1 WHAT WOULD YOU USE TO CLEAN OUT A PONY'S FEET?

a) A body brush

b) A hoof pick

c) A curry comb

2 WHAT IS THE MOST IMPORTANT THING TO WEAR WHEN RIDING?

a) A pair of cream jodhpurs

b) A plain sweatshirt

c) A skull cap

3   WHAT SHOULD YOU ALWAYS MAKE SURE YOUR PONY HAS IN ITS STABLE WHEN YOU BRING IT IN FOR THE NIGHT?

a) A nice view
b) Fresh water and hay
c) Smart rugs ready to put on

4   WHAT SHOULD YOU DO IF YOU THINK YOUR PONY IS POORLY?

a) Tell a responsible adult so they can call a vet
b) Tell your friends
c) Give it a few hours, to see if it gets better

5   WHAT IS AN APPALOOSA PONY?

a) A pony with a triangles on its coat

b) A pony with squares on its coat

c) A pony with spots on its coat

6   WHAT DO YOU USE TO FASTEN A SADDLE IN PLACE?

a) A girth

b) A head collar

c) A martingale

7   WHAT TREATS ARE PONIES ALLOWED?

a) Biscuits

b) Crisps

c) Carrots

8 WHEN YOU ARE RIDING, WHAT SHOULD YOUR FEET BE DOING?

a) Heels down

b) Toes down

c) Moving about as much as possible

9 WHAT IS THE MOST IMPORTANT THING TO THINK ABOUT WHEN APPROACHING A CROSS POLE?

a) Speed – the faster you go, the higher you'll jump

b) Aim for the middle and look forwards

c) Drop the reins so the pony can do its own thing

10 WHAT IS THE MOST IMPORTANT THING TO LOOK FOR IN A RIDING SCHOOL PONY?

a) Good looks to win in the show ring

b) Speed and ability to win gymkhana races

c) A kind and willing temperament

ANSWERS TO THE QUIZ!

Answers: 1b, 2c, 3b, 4a, 5c, 6a, 7c, 8a, 9b, 10c